23

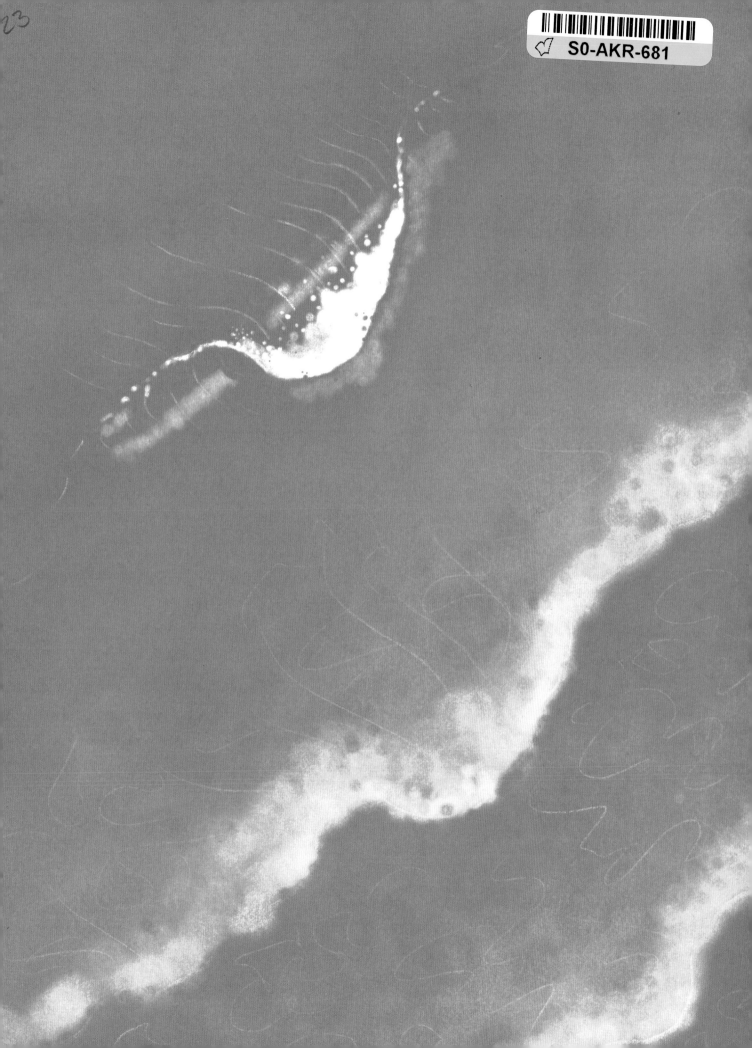

For Megan, Sarah, Chelsea, and James

For those who find themselves, as I have, tumbling in
their own wave, and for those who travel alongside us
and wait for us to come ashore

Published by Roaring Brook Press

Roaring Brook Press is a division of Holtzbrinck Publishing Holdings Limited Partnership

120 Broadway, New York, NY 10271 • mackids.com

Copyright © 2023 by Tyler Charlton. All rights reserved.

Our books may be purchased in bulk for promotional, educational, or business use. Please contact your local bookseller or the
Macmillan Corporate and Premium Sales Department at (800) 221-7945 ext. 5442
or by email at MacmillanSpecialMarkets@macmillan.com.

Library of Congress Control Number: 2022920235

First edition, 2023
Book design by Mina Chung
The art for this book was made with pencil on toned paper and digital painting.
Printed in China by Hung Hing Off-set Printing Co. Ltd., Heshan City, Guangdong Province

ISBN 978-1-250-84203-9

1 3 5 7 9 10 8 6 4 2

THE
WAVE

TYLER CHARLTON

Roaring Brook Press • New York

The last time it happened I was building a fort.

Sometimes . . .

I lose my joy and I don't know why . . .

. . . and the wave takes me away.

I don't see it coming. I never do.

And here I go . . .

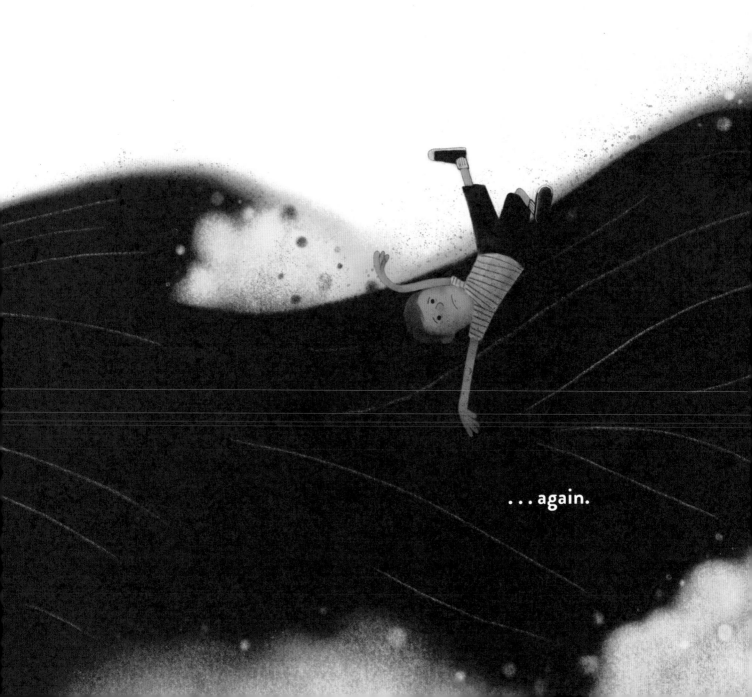

. . . again.

It makes me mad and sad all at the same time
and I want to run away . . .

. . . but you can't outrun a wave.

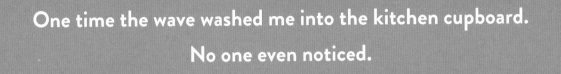
One time the wave washed me into the kitchen cupboard.
No one even noticed.

Didn't they see the wave take me away?

Sometimes I think they did see it, because after a while,
someone handed me a graham cracker.

All I can do is take care of myself until it passes.

I guard my head and my heart
and I watch out for things that can hurt me.

One time I didn't guard my heart. I let it harden . . .
and I said some mean things.

I didn't care.

It felt good to be mad . . .

But I hurt my friend.

Sometimes, I feel all alone.

I miss my joy.

But I've learned that the water will eventually calm.

And the gentle current will begin to carry me
back to the shore.

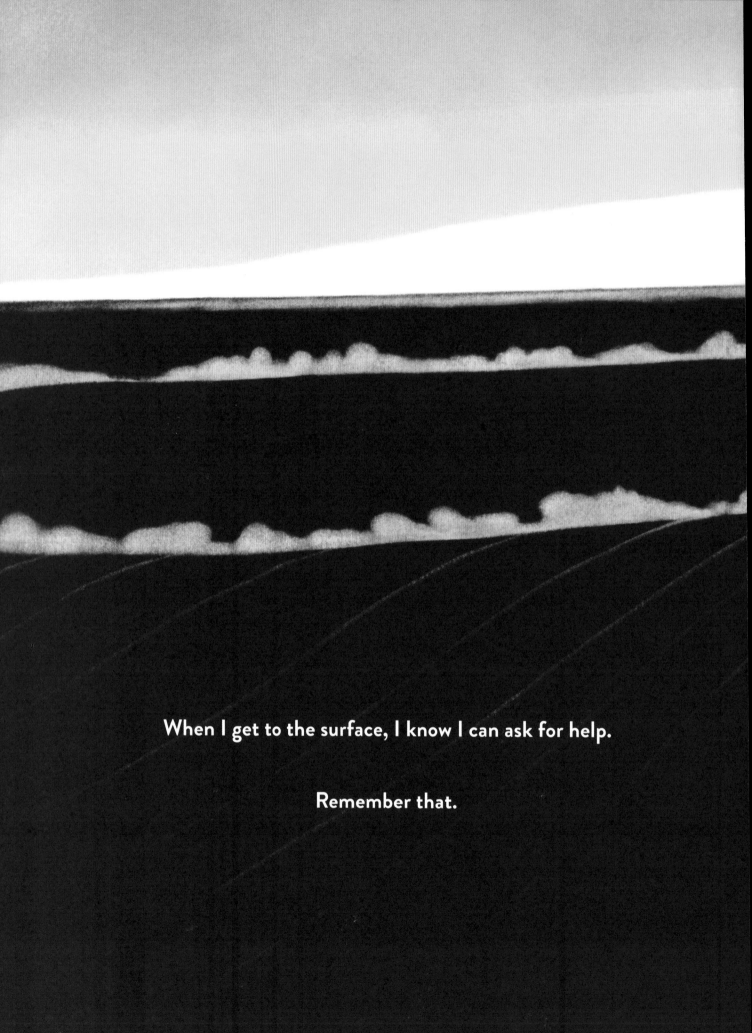

When I get to the surface, I know I can ask for help.

Remember that.

And even though

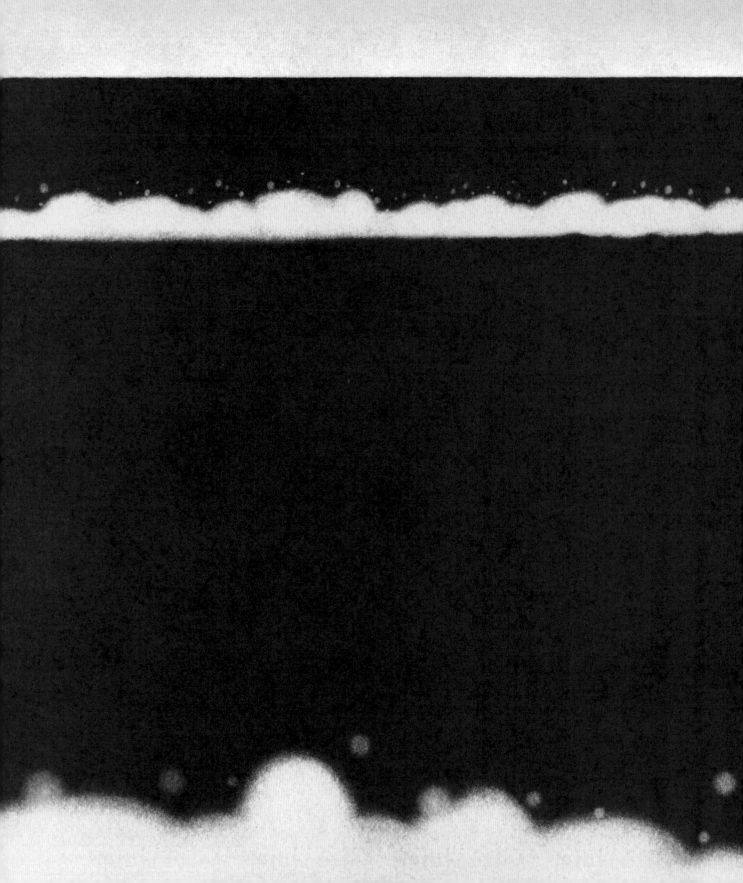

the wave still has me . . .

I can get to my feet.

The wave pulls the sand out from under me
and tries to hold me, but I keep moving.

Remember that.

Keep moving.

Have a soft heart.

Look for the shore.

Keep moving.

And you'll make it through.

AUTHOR'S NOTE

The idea for this book came to me as I was drawing in my sketchbook. I was feeling despair, which is a frustrating and painful kind of sadness where one feels no hope. I don't remember if I knew why I felt this way. I don't always know why. I do know that it's hard for me and it's hard for my friends and my family. I wanted it to stop . . . but I couldn't make it stop. And I didn't think people understood, because when you hurt on the inside, other people can't see it or imagine it for themselves.

However, I remembered feeling this way many times before in my life, both as a child and as a grown-up, and I remembered that it eventually goes away.

As a child, I would play in the Pacific Ocean, and when a huge wave would knock me down and tumble me around and around, I would be helpless to fight it. But I knew if I could stay calm, try to cover my head with my arms, and wait for it to be over, I would eventually be able to stand back up and keep playing. I learned to always remain calm in the Wave.

While I was feeling sad, I drew a picture in my sketchbook of a boy tumbling, looking helpless and without control. But I knew he was waiting for the Wave to pass. And then a surprising thing happened: This drawing started to make me happy. Because after all these years, I finally had a way to show myself and others what was happening on the inside . . . and it was a reminder to myself to remain calm.

It was a little drawing that turned into an illustration that then turned into this book for all of you—to help you notice and find your way out of the Wave sooner rather than later. And if you're on the outside and experience someone you love quietly withdrawing, I hope this helps you notice they might be in the Wave, too.

RESOURCES

Over the years, I've learned that there are steps I can take to get out of the Wave sooner. The first thing to do when you're stuck in the Wave is simply to notice it, which as a grown-up still takes me a while to figure out. But once I've found a foothold and remember that the Wave won't last, I know I can find my path to the shore.

These are the steps I've learned for myself:

▲ **Have a soft heart.** Feelings change. Being mad feels good, but it can hurt the people who love you and want to help you. I try to tell them I'm in the Wave and I'm stuck. I've found that people care and will help or wait patiently for me to feel better. We are not alone.

◆ **Look for the shore.** I remind myself that it's happened before and it didn't last forever. I *will* feel better eventually.

■ **Keep moving.** I move my body. Exercise. Play. Walk. Have an adventure. Build or make something. I even make drawings of how I feel—like drawing a boy tumbling in a wave.

● **Notice the Wave. Have a soft heart. Look for the shore. Keep moving.**

Remember that.

WEBSITES FOR MORE INFORMATION

Adolescent Depression Awareness Program (mADAP), hopkinsmedicine.org/apps/all-apps/madap

Cognitive Behavioral Therapy (CBT) Tools for Youth, therapistaid.com/therapy-worksheets/cbt/adolescents

Erika's Lighthouse, erikaslighthouse.org

Substance Abuse and Mental Health Services Administration (SAMHSA), samhsa.gov

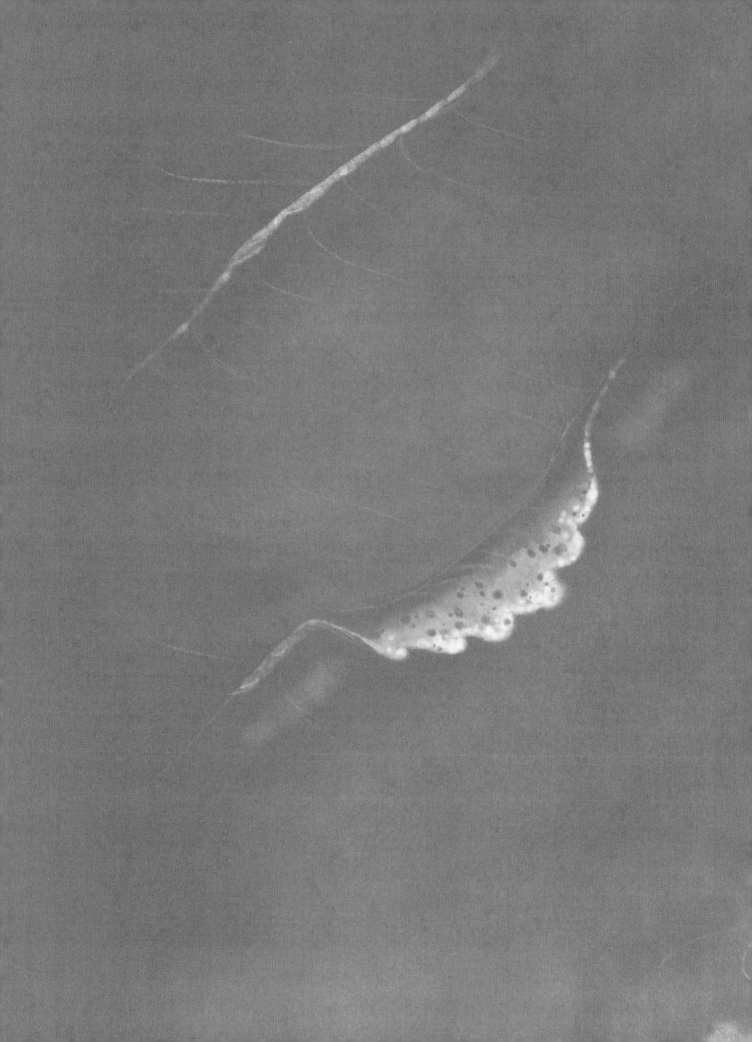